THE RECONSTRUCTION OF MEMORY

TALES OF PRAGUE

THE RECONSTRUCTION OF MEMORY

TALES OF PRAGUE

ALENA GOLDBERG

This is a work of fiction. All of the characters, organizations and events portrayed in this novel are used either fictitiously or are products of the author's imagination.

THE RECONSTRUCTION OF MEMORY
TALES OF PRAGUE

ISBN 978-1-7353624-5-8

For the Velvet Revolution and President Vaclav Havel

INTRODUCTION

The inspiration for writing the book was my own life under the totalitarian regime of former Czechoslovakia filled with emotional and existential difficulties. It is a memory revisited, reconstructed, rethought and rewritten. The characters of the novel search in their memories for something or somebody; their lives merge together and fall apart. Some of them look desperately for the truth, often deeply buried in the society's injustice or the lies of individuals. Not surprisingly, they find themselves in on-going conflicts between their own emotions and reasoning while resisting the pressures of excessive powers, if sexual or political. They struggle to define and achieve their personal or political freedom, often at high costs.

PROLOGUE

I am crying for the loss of my love, for the loss of my freedom, for the loss of the past that is still not forgotten. Where are our loves and the freedom we had fought for? Walking against the current, against contentment, against ourselves is what we do now. What are we doing walking away from our own reality? On the other hand, just think about it, a twitch in the corner of his lips and you are falling in love again. It is like a single leaf on the tree you just happen to look at. An ordinary leaf and then a light breeze blows on it, making it move slightly and beautifully in the way you always remember. It is the feeling of freedom you get, walking through your dark cave of ignorance when suddenly a bright stripe of sunlight begins to lighten your path. You always remember that. Like a mystical force of nature, it transcends your understanding to the higher realms of knowledge. It opens your mind and fills your heart with that strong desire to go and get what you have always wanted: love, freedom, the meaning of your life and the understanding of how to live. You will strive for it, you will search for it or even fight for it and you will find it.

PART ONE

Vera 1978

RED OCTOBER IN PRAGUE

Karl turns his head towards me: "Here, here is the place." They call it White Mountain. Decaying yellow patches of grass below the old pear trees are partially covered by the red and gold leaves of October. Today, everything reminds me of something else. October, falling leaves, golden yellow on blood red; it feels like an image from a history lesson: Petersburg's Golden Winter

Palace in 1917 during the Russian Revolution, shooting and stabbing with the blood red flags above. Thinking about violence often brings to my mind the only type of love making I have remembered. It is the push and shove, the struggle between a master and a slave. I keep asking myself why I am here with Karl who keeps persuading me for almost a year to have sex with him. He is my friend from the past. We grew up on the same street of a poor working class neighborhood, too close to each other to ever date or marry. Eventually, we drifted apart and married our dates, but later became close colleagues at work. Karl was ambitious and quickly climbed to a high position. He often boasted how he had cheated on his wife with his female boss to be promoted. He has managed to have sex with many women outside his marriage without any commitment. Just for the freedom of it, as he says. Anyway, I think cheating is like treachery and is wrong and disgusting. Not that I care about it much, not any more. My husband is barely here. His job and his slutty behavior have taken him away from me. Still, I do not want to be a traitor like him or Karl. It is not my choice, though one should be free to choose if not harming the other. I took this existentialist belief for my own, in order to at least sense some freedom since in the reality it does not exist. "Let's free ourselves", Karl suddenly proclaims loudly with his propagandist style of shouting messages to the masses, "Let's be free from our obligations! Sex is an act of freedom"! I resent this talk of banal persuasion, it is embarrassing. Besides that, I believe that actual freedom could be achieved only through an active resistance.

I am deep in my thoughts, walking along and ignoring Karl when all of a sudden he oversteps me, stopping on the front of me. He grabs my shoulder with his right hand, his left squeezes my waist. Slowly, he forces my body to the ground. My knees begin to tremble. I cannot handle this unexpected feeling of fatigue that overwhelms my body stiffening under his physical pressure. My mind switches off and I am out of my reality. "Are you a party member?" I ask him instead of fighting against his force. "I love you", he whispers into my ear. "Stop it! Are you involved with the communist party? " I shout now. There is no reply. His redden eyes look into mine, his whole face is laughing at me. I am trapped in a loveless embrace. I cannot run away; I cannot move anymore. Karl is on top of me, his legs are now between mine and his eyes stare blindly into my frightened face. He yells at me: "What's wrong with you? What for all those questions? Let it go! You know that I have obligations to my family. We want to travel abroad and I want to finish my engineering degree. We will need a bigger apartment. Yes, yes, yes, I need the party; I have to be a member! I am a member! We all are party members one way or another. Remember Vera, you live in this shit too, you must try to adapt. I do not dictate the politics, I am not the master". He takes a deep breath and continues to intimidate me with his loud voice: "Forget your stupid dreams of freedom and remember that you

10

are here a slave for life. Return to your reality, everybody in this country is a communist with or without the party membership. There is no difference between us". "Come on now, sweetie", he controls his anger for a while, "Why so many questions? Do not make me to force you. I want to give you this freedom now. We may not be here tomorrow".

My mind is busy with recollections; my thoughts just wonder, leaving my body unguarded. This garden on White Mountain had once belonged to somebody. Children used to fly kites here, lovers went for long walks through the orchard and families had picnics on the top of the mountain. I too used to come here as a child with my family and later mostly on my own. It was long after the government confiscated this property. It became, in its terms, everybody's land, but for me, it was a land of nobody, a magical place. I used to run down on the dramatically sloping hillside to the narrow piece of land which divided the hill from the shoulder of the river Vltava. Watching the fishermen on their small boats struggling against the strong current, my eyes ran with the strong wide silvery river. It was jumping over the big rocks, moving swiftly from one side of the bank to another in its s-shape snake like move, flowing forwards with its natural power and finally disappearing with the hissing sound in the distance. I have loved my river, my river Vltava. Sitting by its bank for a while, I then climbed slowly back to the top of the hill. I am like Sisyphus, I thought, reaching the mountain's peak and running down again, like Sisyphus, a slave to his destiny, rolling his stone uphill for eternity. I came to the mountain top, devastated when I was not admitted to the university because of the family's political view. It was time to cope with the harsh reality of my life. My father's anti-communist pro-democratic views were enough for being alienated by the current political system. Teens like me were destined to become unskilled workers or, at the best, trained laborers. By publicly rejecting the "undesirable" political views and joining the communist party, many would better their chances to higher education and easier lives. Some of them had justified such actions by their intentions only to use the party, not really believing in its agenda. I was not ready for that. I believed in the truth, I desired to live in it. I wanted to have life without lies. I was searching for the truth, desperately, even though I have already carried its meaning in my name Vera. But the truth I found was different than I expected. It was devaluated by opportunism and cowardice. People around me have continued to live with their eyes shut. They lost their identities and become mere imitations of their repressive masters. They were slowly developing into robots, perfect social realist creations that no longer needed the truth. They chose to live in their dark caves of ignorance and agreed with their jailers. Only a few stood upright from time to time and resisted the oppression, but were broken down, their efforts becoming fruitless. So far, all of those struggles for freedom have ended with political rapes.

"Karl, please, no!" I am shouting now, "I do not like you, you fucking asshole, you hypocrite! Do not touch me. Leave me alone! Leave me alone! Let me go! Please let me go!" I feel numbed not knowing what is going to happen next. It is like fainting, but I am trying to get my mind back to set control over my numbed body. It does not work. My mind is elsewhere, derailed. There are flashes from the past that obscure my rationality: red scarves around the necks of young communists, Greek sculptures turning into statues of Lenin; my father is taken to jail. People are greeting the WWII liberating Soviet Army but the date says it is 1968, the Russian occupation of Czechoslovakia. I am there, only sixteen years old and must learn how to make homemade bombs. There is a lot of blood in this resistance, my mind and body is injured. My friend is dying on the street of Prague. But it is the first of May 1948, the Workers' Day and young communists are walking with a great joy in a parade on the street, singing, ignoring the fatally wounded man.

I am back now. I force my body to react. I am kicking and try to scratch and hit. It does not work for me. Karl is holding my arms behind my back so I cannot fight him. He is pushing my body down to the ground with all his weight. I am helpless pinned to the ground. My overcoat is open, its buttons gone. He is ripping off my dress and my stockings, his pants are half down to his hips, his chest is pressuring my breasts. He is going to rape me! I see him reaching to his crotch but as he lifts his chest a bit from mine, he lets off my right arm, tightly tucked until now behind my back. With all my strength I get my arm from behind my back and free the left arm too to poke my finger deep into my torturer's right eye. He reacts by a violent scream lifting his body completely away from mine and reaches with both of his hands to his face. This moment is enabling me to roll quickly aside from his body, rise to my feet and run away from him. I am running fast, faster and faster towards the edge of the White Mountain. I am terrified that he is speeding after me and will get me. Petrified,

I slip, stumble and fall. I feel sharp pain after hitting the ground hard. My knee and my shoulder hurt and I am rolling fast down the sloping hill towards the river Vltava. The ground is rough and slippery and I am rolling down like a rock, unable to stop. Instinctively, I manage to cover at least part of my face with my arms, but my body is exposed to the rocky terrain of the mountain. I sense my freedom from Karl, but I am afraid I may die here. My wounded body stops at the edge of the water. I lay here helplessly. I do not know if I can move or do not want to move. I see fast running water on the front of my eyes and hear the sound of the strong current of my favored river, hissing like a snake, jumping over the boulders playfully. I feel I am being carried away with it, far away towards the horizon under the bridges of my city to a place I have never been before. It makes me happy. I close my eyes and everything stops.

TWO PIGEONS

I am driving home, thinking of Vera, imagining her face: Vera smiling, waving at me, Vera talking to her co-workers, Vera giving speech on working environment in the company cafeteria, Vera smoking a cigarette over a cup of coffee, looking directly into my eyes. Vera, Vera, Vera how much more is hidden inside of you? I have to visit you. I need to talk to you. I am falling in love with you. I am turning around, now driving in the opposite direction away from my home. I hope her husband is not there, passes my mind as I am turning towards her apartment in the panel housing project.

An empty space of the Red Square is gloomy in the approaching twilight. A drunkard is laying face down on the sidewalk at the east corner. As my car moves closer to the person, I can see it is a woman, a young woman looking remarkably like Vera. She is lying there motionless. She may be hurt or dead. I hesitate to get out of the car but drive closer to the sidewalk. "Oh, my God, it is Vera! What the hell had happened to her? She is not moving!"

He can see now her torn wet clothes and bloody scrapes on her body. Out of the car in no time, he is picking her up to his arms. "Hug me, please, I am so cold", she opens her eyes and babbles while he is putting her down onto the back seat of his Renault.

18

"Vera, Verushka, this is not you as I know you, your strong confident self. Vera, where is your spark that always shines out of you? Your body is cold, is that what left of you? Your dress is soaking wet, you are feverish. Are you in pain? What happened to you?" He keeps asking her, but she is not answering, just mumbles something incomprehensibly, shivering on the back seat of the car. The vulnerability of the situation gives him the courage he had never had before, to show his compassion and love for her. "I want to help you to feel better, warm you up, to heel your wounds. I am genuinely worrying about you." He gets quickly to the back seat to be with her and begin to caress her hair gently. He embraces her tightly to warm her up and she clings to him. Vera feels wounded, hurt, scared and she wants warmth and love. It is happening too fast. He is not used to it. She hugs him back and put her face close to his. He begins to kiss her wet face with patches of blood still on it, caresses her limp soaked hair and reaches for her swollen lips with his. Wrapping his warm body

19

around her wounded one, he kisses her passionately. He feels uplifted in the body and mind, careless of where they are or who may see them in this loving sexual embrace. The urge and longing to be close to someone, to be touched, to bring oneself closer to love comes so spontaneously to both of them. "As in the moment of a daydream, you just appeared to me, falling straight to my arms, you wounded, wonderful angel. Do not go back to your distant eternity, stay with me in this life, this reality. I am your safety, your Earth. I am your guardian, my earthly angel". He is saying all this thoughts aloud to her, but she may not hear it. She is out of her earthly realm already.

The darkness falls slowly, like a heavy theater curtain on the end of the show when everybody is leaving and soon be gone. The climax is gone, the play is over, the applause of the rapidly moving eye lids slowed down. The closeness is over. Sadness overwhelms him as he looks out through the car's windshield and sees two pigeons watching them.

I have no idea what had happened to me after my fall into the river or how did I get on the back seat of Misha's car, but I am alive and do not want to think what may have happened. I do not want to think at all. We are in a passionate embrace. "You must have been half unconscious when I found you on this street corner. You were laying face down. What happened to you?" he asks me, leaning over my battered body partially covered by my wet clothing. My whole body aches but I feel warm heeling coming from the inside me as Misha strokes my hair. "It is getting late." I say, seeing his lips trying to reach for mine again. I have to go. Like a Cinderella from her prince, I am quickly turning away from him and pushing my way out of the car. Everything hurts; something happened to me but I still cannot recall beyond the river fall. I have some kind of amnesia and the constant ringing in my ears does not let me to concentrate and think. It feels like a new beginning, resurrection, new life... I am on the street still close to Misha's car. I must look homeless in the oversized Misha's jacket he wrapped me in. It makes me smile a little and I turn my head with a thank you on my mind towards his car. I can see him looking out through the windshield. That little twitch on his lips and the spark in his eyes are still there. I turn away and walk as fast as I can, holding my pain in. When I turn around towards the car for the second time I do not see his face in the window anymore. The car is almost invisible in the darkness that fell and the silence that surrounds it as if in suspended motion. A moment like this...

I am getting closer to my apartment in the panel housing. It is very dark outside now, but the street lamps are not lit yet, a normal thing in our sickly governed society. I am afraid of the unexpected and hold the house keys between the fingers of my closed right fist ready to defend myself, in the case someone attacks me. I must be a bit paranoid after all. Thankfully, I am at home now and I am OK.

Only now I can recall what happened to me on the White Mountain. It is a scattered memory: Karl, the sexual violence to alienate my body, my escape of the rape, the fall, the pain and despair are slowly replayed in my mind. I feel confused, disgusted and ashamed, my stomach turns up and I vomit in the bathroom. I still feel nauseous and sit on the sofa, starring motionlessly through the balcony window into the dark. My dog Arrack is not sitting next to me tonight. He has gone with my estranged husband to wherever he went tonight. I am looking into the dark night for a long time. This life here is frightening. I have no personal or social freedom. I live in the society which domain is the political and sexual domination. People around me replicate this violence. What am I going to do? How can I live here so alienated, my spirit diminished, my hopes gone? I get up and put a record on the turntable. "We've Gotta Get Out of this Place", sing The Animals. I close my eyes, but my mind cannot rest. I think of Sisyphus rolling his stone up to the hill for eternity and Abebi Bikila crossing the final line of his winning marathon run. It is time for me to start my own race to victory. I will leave this country as soon as I can.

INCHES APART

I am sitting in the company cafeteria smoking a cigarette over my awfully tasting instant coffee. It is a couple of days after I found Vera on the street. I wanted to talk to her about my plan but decided to write it to her instead. She sits alone at a long cantina table, close enough to me to gaze time to time into my eyes. She is again her strong self.

Dear Vera! My whole life felt into pieces, there is nothing I can do to solve this broken puzzle. My wife is leaving me for someone else and I want to start a new life, but not here. Come with me to Austria, wonderful angel, I need you. I will make you happy. We will solve a new puzzle together. We will make our own map for the journey through our lives. I want to go for a ride with you, for a long ride... wherever it will take us. Please come with me.

I am going to give her my message tonight, I decide, and put the writing for now into my jeans pocket.

I need you, my guardian, Vera says to herself looking into Misha's eyes across the distance. With you, life could be a beautiful ride. I need you, my friend, to come with me somewhere, anywhere. I have to tell you tonight. I will be leaving this country really soon.

The black Renault is parked near the Czech border crossing to Austria. "Let's not cross here, I have a bad feeling about this one. After the struggle we had on the way with the broken tire now the long line before the border gate. Let's go to Gmund crossing, it is smaller, feels better." "You are crazy, Vera", replies Misha but follows the advice of his former supervisor.

We are pretending to leave Czechoslovakia for only a weekend trip, with just some pocket money in Austrian currency and falsified documents in our pockets. But we are not coming back. I am excited but scared at the same time as we drive towards our freedom. My watch shows exactly 4:20 PM when we finally cross the border to Austria. It was not easy. Still on the Czech side of the border, we were searched thoroughly, car and all. I was body searched. My vagina was searched by a fascistically looking female comrade. After back home, it meant nothing to me.

It is a sunny day today. The fields in the Austrian countryside are greener than back at home, the meadows smell fresh, perfumed by the scent of the fragile April flowers. The small pasture we are sitting on is still looking wintery, but patches of the fresh bright green grass are springing up here and there. The tiny white flowers of the early spring stick their heads towards the sky, moving gently in the light breeze. We are in a fairytale country. Finally here, across the border, the world feels a new and bright and so does our future. Misha is busy opening a bottle of champagne that we saved for this moment. It is hard to believe that we are here free to make something good of our lives. I feel like shouting goodbye towards the distant Czechoslovakian border that we just left behind, but I am afraid to disturb the tranquility of this calm foreign country. Cheers, we are raising our paper cups filled with the foaming liquid. It is for the first time, since our decision to emigrate, that we are not tense and worried. Back at home in Prague, no one knows that we are not coming back. But all that is yesterday and it is quickly disappearing behind us. The present is ours and the future will be wonderful; we are sure of it. Our confidence in it seems to rise with the level of alcohol in our blood. Drinking in silence, my thoughts wonder to the two ancient cities, which, like two sisters, me and Eva, are divided by barb wire fences: Vienna and Prague.

How much I have already suffered without her, runs through my head. I have never before realized what it means to me to be a father. She is only a year old, how could I leave her behind like this, my little baby? I do feel the pain of the night when I found her mother with another guy making love on our new sofa. I left in anger and promised to myself to never come back, never. How could I forget about my baby angel sleeping peacefully in her room, giving myself this promise?

The rain plays waltz on the roof of the black Renault. "It makes beautiful music." I say. Misha does not say anything, but he too seems to be thinking of something. His face is pale, his lips tight close. His eyes are looking sternly through the wet window shield. There is no spark in them. "How much I have loved her?" he says suddenly aloud. "Are you thinking about your daughter?" I ask him back in the quiet gentle voice, hoping he does not mean his wife. I know he loves his daughter very much and must miss her. As he turns his boyish face towards me, I can see now, there are tears in his eyes. "No!" His eyes look in mine rather aggressively: "I am thinking what will happen to us from now on. We are here so alone, so helpless with no friends". He still holds the gearshift stiffly, although he stopped the car almost an hour ago. It makes me fear that he may just turn around and drive back to where we came from. I am trying to move closer to embrace him but feel his resentment. So I take his hand gently away from the gearshift. "Misha, we will have to try hard, once we secured, to get your baby daughter abroad, we will do all we can to make it possible, will contact those who had helped us with our documents. There must be a way. But I hope you realize that your wife will have to come as well". Misha calms down but his expression shows pain. I am now holding his face in my hands, looking into his eyes for a moment before I lean closer to kiss him. Sadness and a feeling of fatigue overwhelm me. As I look at his face, so closed to mine, it blurs away before my eyes. We are so close, yet, so far apart. I feel as sorry for him as I feel angry because I know he loves me and will exchange this love for his fatherly one. It is natural for him to feel this way, I think. Still, it is shocking and painful to me. I have always felt like an older sister to him and tried to protect him, asking him questions and answering them for him too. But I wanted him to be my guardian, my lover. He ought to choose his own happiness, but now I need his love and do not want to lose him yet. Misha moves the gearshift and steps on the gas. We are driving towards Vienna.

I am exhausted and worries come to me. We have had a plan; we have wanted to solve our new puzzle of life. Why is this doubt obstructing our future? Why are we drifting apart so soon? I close my eyes in the attempt to go away from all of this and fall asleep.

We walk hand in hand through the fairy tale countryside until we reach a beautiful city. There is a café in the ancient part of the city, next to the cathedral and we found a table by the window with the view of the church. We smile at each other, drinking wine. My glass suddenly turns into a large challis and we hold it together like a Holy Grail, now entering the cathedral. Our wish to get married is granted by a priest and us, now a married couple, run to our little room in the attic of a townhouse. The room is high up above all the city rooftops where only the pigeons can watch us making love.

Sadly, it is only a dream. I know that this will never happen. I just made up my mind to break up with Misha to prevent him from leaving me first. I am angry but sad. I hate losing a game before it starts. Just a bad luck, I guess. It has begun with the broken tire and it is ending with the broken heart.

It is already dark as we get close to Vienna and begins to rain heavily when we arrive to our final destination, the refugee camp in a little town Traiskirchen. Every immigrant to Austria has to go through this camp wherever he or she decides to go afterwards.

With the door wide open, the car is now parked near the gate to what looks like an entry to a garden. The rain gets in, but we are not getting out. Not yet; it is a bit scary to make the first step into the new world of freedom. A solid metal bar fence framed with mature bushes and shrubs connects to a huge green painted iron gate with a sign above that reads Wilkommen. It is closed shut and the large muddy puddle on the front of it makes it impossible to walk forwards without getting soaked. As we sit motionless in the car, just staring at the imposing gate, the continuously pouring rain is filling up and widening the dirty puddle. Through the gap between the fence bars, I can see the empty wet courtyard of the camp. It is a dark place with some wooden buildings in the back and a better brick style house at the front. A small door in one of the distant barracks opens with a cracking sound. Two ghostly figures walk out into the cold rain. As they pass a dim light of the street lamp, I can see they are two men. The taller one bends down to pick something from the ground. Then he seems to put his find into the corner of his mouth and turns towards the shorter man: "Zapal mnie, prosze", says he loudly in Polish that I can understand. A tiny sparks of the cigarette lighter blinks a couple of times in the dark, eventually creating a small flame. It takes time before I can spot the taller of the men puffing out a tiny cloud of smoke while the smaller one keeps looking up at him. Then they walk together towards the back of the courtyard and soon disappear from the sight.

Misha and I get finally out of the car and stare into the fenced yard without doing anything except getting soaked and wet. After a while of this torture, I get some courage and press the door bell on the small wall next to the gate connected to the fence. Misha does the same a couple more times after me. From a dimly lit room of the brick house near the gate emerge two older men dressed in military uniforms with rifles over their shoulders and proceed towards the gate. With a terribly loud screeching sound, the gate opens. "Gutten Aben. Wir bitten um Asyl" both of us ask in German almost in one voice. It is a sentence we learned ahead of coming here, a kind of a password to all immigrants seeking asylum. "Ja, ja. Gutten Abend, bitte komm herein, aber achtung! ", greets us an unnecessarily loud voice of one of them inviting us harshly into our new home. We walk swiftly across the large muddy puddle on the front of the gate that extends far beyond it, the only way to get in. It is deep, dirty and cold. We are not welcomed, flashes through my brain. It is like entering a prison.

Even more depressing image of an open gate to a concentration camp comes to mind as I am marching through the gate with the Wilkommen sign above, splashing the filthy water all over my legs in my new shoes. It feels freezing and uncomfortable walking in my now totally drenched pumps. My mind cannot rest; it is getting crazy. The images of Jewish prisoners entering the gate of the concentration camp are now being replaced by the ancient Jews crossing the Red Sea from the Egyptian slavery to their freedom. This imagery of freedom makes me feel a bit more hopeful about the happy future that for a moment seemed so far away. I need to be victorious and I know how to keep my direction. I will keep marching, I will be brave. Vera, someone had said to me a long ago, the world is inside of you not around you, so do not be afraid. I am not, but I do not know if freedom begins like this: suffocating you first, knocking you down to your knees, trying to strip you down of your dignity. I think it may be. It will not trust you until the day you stand up strong in your own rights and say ENOUGH, realizing that you are a free person and have the rights to pursue your own happiness. One day, the people back at home in Prague will understand that as well and say ENOUGH to their oppressors. We are always just inches apart from our own freedom.

VERA IS GONE

A little girl stands on a river shore. It is my sister Eva. I see her wet face clearly as my row boat passes her. "Vera, do not leave me here, come back!" calls Eva loudly. I feel like crying while my boat moves rapidly away from her. I was supposed to take care of her, but I left her behind, waiting. Perhaps one day I will come back to you. I turn my eyes away from Eva who is quickly fading off before my eyes. I am alone in the boat that has no oars. The current is very strong, rocking the boat wildly and I am afraid I may drown. The only thing left for me to do is to lie down inside the boat and let the river carry me on. It is moving forward pretty fast towards the west and out of the city. I can see some islands, then a couple of Baroque churches with shiny roofs and golden domes. Then comes the forest; it is dark, dense with fir trees; its ground is completely black, covered by blueberry bushes with ripe berries. I see my little sister Eva again. She stands on the edge of the forest, hugging an empty mug close to her chest. Her mouth is wide open, stained by the blueberry juice. I remember filling up her mug with blueberries during our forest outings, while she was only eating them. How will she manage without me? Eva just stands there, her eyes gazing into a distance. She does not call me, does not cry but stand there with that widely open mouth, like a figure from the painting by Edward Munch. Could she even see me hiding inside my row boat? I watch her until she disappears again from my sight. A strange feeling of sickness overcomes me. I am passing White Mountain, my Mountain Sisyphus, as I call it. I see the pear orchard on the top of the hill. "Bye Sisyphus, goodbye my mountain!" I call, knowing I will not see it again. The river is louder than my voice now, passing some large boulders in its turn. It jumps over or zigzags around them, hissing like a big snake. I see a young woman, looking remarkably like me, lying face up in the shallow water near the shore. I want to call her not to stay there for too long, the river is cold and treacherous here, and she could drown, but I am late to warn her. The current here is strong and my boat speeds up, violently rocking towards a city in the distance. I can see very attractive Renaissance buildings flanking the river promenade. People are coming out of the doors of the buildings and crossing the equally beautiful bridges above me. There are more and more bridges passing me. It makes my head spin looking upward to their arches that moves above me like a fast forwarded movie. How many more bridges it will take to leave you my city? I am now laughing violently to cover up my fears and the urge to cry.

Vera is gone. He opens the white curtain covering the glass door to the balcony. Some dirty wet spots, a reminder of the February snow, still remain in the corners of its tiled floor. He recalls the sunny deck he had seen in his favored design magazine. They both tried to turn this pathetic looking balcony into something magnificent. It has never turned that way. Empty wishes! One cannot live in illusion full of empty wishes; it is only a belief that counts. There was no belief. The red colored electric grill is now filled with filthy water from the melted snow and the empty flower pots are hidden under the branches of the last Christmas tree. Vera's old rocking chair is still here, dirty and wet like an abandoned baby. It lost its purpose without her. Jaroslav remembers their first dates. She was young and inexperienced but with mind of her own, a very serious mind it was. It stayed with her during their marriage. She was a damn good looking, but much too serious and studious for him. That was why later on he started to look for fun with other women. He was never there for her. He knew that. When she had an emergency appendectomy, he was skiing with his lover in Slovakia. Her miscarriage almost killed her when she was waiting for him in vain to join her for a vacation. He does not remember why he did not come to join her. There was no need for remorse or guilt because he knew he loved her anyway. He still loves her and will love her forever. Yes, his sometimes violent streaks were bad, but it happens in many good families. Her broken nose is fixed and no one can recognize anything. She asked me for a divorce, maybe to be able to marry a better man. Silly goose, she had no clue she could be in a polyamorous relationship if she asked. She was so faithful to her old fashion ideals. I have loved her and I have wanted to keep her, Jaroslav says to himself. "But this is the end of it!" he continues aloud in an annoyed tone of voice, closing the balcony door before the dog that was there could come inside the room. Arrack barks and scratches the dirty glass balcony door. Of course, he has never liked to be left alone, Vera's Dalmatian, just like her. He was a gift for her, a pretty cute puppy. She used to ask jokingly if it was a substitute for a baby. Never really appreciated this expensive present, took it, loved it and now left it behind, he speaks to himself. Jaroslav lets the dog in the living room and passionately pets his head. "She left you, buddy. She did not love you. How could she do this to you? How could she do this to us? It should not happen to me". He looks out to the muddy street of the panel housing complex. A couple of school children dressed in raincoats run through the large puddle in the middle of the unfinished road. This was supposed to be the so called academic city, a suburban project he was part of, the place where the dreams of perfect living come true. It meant to be an architectural achievement for the elite. It is now buried in the middle of the cheap panel housing project. "Fuck, the five-year plan is over and they did not even manage to finish the road", Jaroslav thinks aloud again and sinks into the sofa by the window. It got sunny outside for a while, before the rain returned. "Crazy weather, up and down, just like her", he now screams towards the frightened dog that is running away from him, "She has never made up her mind, hot and cold, smiling and crying at once. Stupid Vera, stupid crazy women, they are all the same!" He gets up from the sofa and walks mindlessly back and forth in the living room. Then, he begins to cry. Vera is gone.

PART TWO

Adella 1968

TRAM NUMBER 10

The Russian invasion is over, but the Soviet occupants stay. The people's efforts for a better life and government during the political movement called Prague Spring are broken and so is my relationship with my true love, my first love.

Tram number 10 is moving slowly to the station Crossroads, the working class borrow of Prague. Already from the distance, I can see it is packed. Nevertheless, I pick up my small travel bag from the sidewalk and begin to cross the road towards the tram platform. It just stopped but only the front door next to the driver opens. It is completely full but I have to get in anyway and so begin to squeeze myself up and onto the already occupied first step. I continue to press my body, now more aggressively, against those on the front of me. That happens every single day I travel on a tram; I have to manage to get inside the overcrowded vehicle no matter what, because its arrival intervals are just too long. There is no space for my duffel bag, so I have to hold it tightly between my calves. As always, nobody protests against my aggressiveness, on the contrary, all the sweaty bodies surrounding me are familiar with such a routine and remain motionless, the saturnine faces above continue to smile slightly. Dear God, I think, comradeship is now firmly established. How pathetic, only four month ago, these bodies were alive. We were brothers and sisters. Many of us were throwing Molotov cocktails onto Russian tanks as easily as we shout at them to scram using our school Russian. For me, it is still alive. I sure remember the tank's turret pointing towards my family apartment window threatening to shoot if anti-occupational posters were not immediately removed from the wall of the building. I have the blood of my friend and the grimace of death on his face still on the front of my eyes. In my dreams, I continue to run away from the Prague Radio Station headquarters that we managed to hold free of occupation until overpowered by a tank unit. I dream that I am running across the Wenceslas Square on front of a Russian tank. I hide from the bullets. The dream feels real, its reality frightening. I know there will not be a democratic state with the permanent settlement of the occupational army. People were forced to go back to their little lives under the tyrannous regime. Again, they have to carry their heavy burdens of the repressed believes and hopes in the heroic Sisyphus way. Craps, enough of that!

It has taken a few stops before the tram spat out the half of the crowd by the Liben shipyard. At least I am able to move ahead a bit and begin to proceed towards the ticket conductor sitting importantly in his high seat at the middle of the tram like some presiding court judge. "Exact change or out", says the man in the grey police style uniform to me sternly before I have a chance to ask him for a ticket. "Hurry up, you are not an only one here, I serve to the whole nation", adds this middle manager in the tone of a dictator. "Here is your 60 cents", I manage to get the wet coins out of my clenched sweaty fist and receive in return equally sweaty piece of a small paper ticket. Only now I am noticing someone's eyes staring at me. He has entered the tram through the middle door labeled Exit as others were leaving the vehicle, ignoring the strict passenger rules and the furious conductor: "Comrade, what are you doing? What do you think? Don't you see the sign Exit? Have some respect of authority!" Not a comrade, I am assessing him. He is elegant, perhaps a decade older than me, well dressed for this time when good merchandise is scarce and good clothing almost unattainable. He has no baggage; one hand in the pocket, the other is reaching leisurely for the handle mounted too high for an average height person to use it. Must be one of us, I am persuading myself. I am pretty sure of that. The persistence of that man looking at me does not bother me much. Men are often eyeing me in this way or are turning their heads after me on the street. I am already used to that and it does not completely displease me, but I keep my distance. Most of the time, I avoid an eye contact with strangers, but occasionally get caught in the game, exchanging flirtatious stare. It is a meaningless game just to kill the boredom of the tram ride. This time, I ignore the intruder of my privacy while being aware of his almost nasty interest to capture my attention. I wonder if I am going to be late for my train to the boarding school. What time is it? I want to look at my wrist watch, but cannot release my arm that is stacked between mine and somebody else's hip. "Grand

Central Station", announces the nasty conductor loudly and a crowd of people pushes through the open doors leaving the tram almost empty. I am jumping off and starting to run towards the beautiful architectural gem across the street that is the train station. It is the Grand Central still known as Wilson Station built in 1920's during the First Republic and dedicated to the US president Woodrow Wilson. The elaborate golden clock in the exterior cornice of the station shows five minutes to twelve. It has shown this time since it had stopped after the Second World War. No one has cared to fix it since. But now I can check the time on my watch. I have barely ten minutes to get on the train but luckily, the ticket line is not very long. "One student to Zbuch please, one way." "The train is boarding, miss, on the platform four." says the ticket clerk friendly as she handles me a small hard cardboard ticket. I lift up my little duffel bag from the beautifully tiled but dirty floor and head towards the underground passage leading to the train platforms. The number four is extremely busy.

A hoard of people is pushing towards the open doors of the train wagons. The same thing again, I am getting a mental picture of how it may look inside: no seats, not even space to stand.

"The next one to Plzen leaves in two hours", I hear from behind me, "do not despair; we can have a drink, waiting for it together, if you like". The man whose face is suddenly on the front mine continues: "It would be a great pleasure to wait for the next train with you, if you allow me to." "I recognize you; we were in the same tram. Did you follow me here?" "No, no, not at all, I was supposed to pick up my brother, but he is not here yet. He will arrive much later", says the man with a confidence of a skillful liar, looking straight into my eyes. "By the way, I am Daniel, Danny and you?" "Adella, please to meet you" I smile at him and extend my hand for the handshake. There is a bar just next to the station, the same architectural wonder and elegance as the train station but quiet and empty. Without saying a word to each other, we slowly walk in. Daniel picks a small round table for two and orders aperitifs for us. Looking into each other's eyes, our tongues immerse in the bitter sweet taste of the drink as well as in a pleasant talk. But the time is going fast, faster than we want it to. We walk together back to the station through the nearby park where Daniel's attempt to kiss me spoils my friendly mood. From that point, we walk faster and far away from each other without a single word. The strong wind starts to pick up and the sky is suddenly getting darker; the clouds, pregnant with moisture, are floating close to the ground. Very slowly, it is starting to snow. This change of the weather pleases me tremendously. It is like a mood swing, like a change of heart. The cold beautiful snowflakes land with a feather touch on my lashes and Daniel's mustache. It brings back a bit of the lost happiness from our short afternoon together. It makes us careless and child-like. We move closer to each other looking up to the sky catching the falling treasure on our faces, on our lips, our eyes, our tongues.

Back in the train station on the platform number four a whistle blows and the steam train begins to move with a speed of a snail, making squeaking noises at first, later replaced by a huffing and puffing and a familiar rhythmical sound of the wheels turning. Daniel stands patiently on the platform and looks into the train window to catch a glimpse of me or get my attention. I am sitting by the window and track him in the corner of my eye so not to look directly in his face. He is about to wave his goodbye, but I am not turning my face towards him, looking stubbornly into the empty seat opposite to me, not a blink of an eye. Anyway, he will be stalking me from now on, I am sure of that. I told him, I come to Prague every two weeks on Friday nights to see my parents. He will be coming to the train station and waiting for me until he catches up with me. He seems to be that kind of a man, a hunter.

Gone goes the train now, away from Prague and the man I do not wish to see again. Without turning my head even a bit towards the platform to see him for the last time, my thoughts goes to Yannek, a soldier, my first love. I am afraid we are breaking apart. He is jailed in the army barracks, punished by those whom he served. He rebelled against his superior's order not to defend the base against the landing occupants. Still, Yannek is my true love; I am imagining his face in my mind but the vision quickly fades.

The train is now moving faster towards the tunnel guarded by a Soviet soldier. I am looking at him from my now open window. His closely shaved face looks happy. The snowflakes fall slowly on his nose, his eyebrows, his hat and shoulders. When the train passes him, he salutes with his right hand, raising his left at the same time and waves to me. He smiles a friendly smile. I do not return his greetings, he is an occupant. It is November 1968 and everything has changed.

TRUE LOVE

It is Saturday, exactly two weeks after I met Daniel. I came to Prague for the weekend to visit my family, but I am already leaving. The first snow had melted into dirty puddles covering Prague's streets and sidewalks. The occupant army has declared a curfew on us. They call us contra revolutionaries. We were supposed to be revolutionaries like comrades Lenin and Stalin, following the footstep of the Russian October Revolution, but we are disobeying to do so. We have to pay for it, they say, we are contras.

I am in the tram number 10 again, going to the Wilson Train Station. It is late at night and I am determined to take the midnight train to Ceske Budejovice if it is still running. I know am disobeying the order given by the Russians but I have to. I decided to visit Yannek, my sweet heart, in the military jail. Notwithstanding the 9 PM curfew, I am out to get this train and going. On Sunday is my last chance to see my boyfriend, my first and true love. As he wrote to me, he will be transferred to a military working camp somewhere else already on Monday. I must see him, he needs me.

"Pokazhe bumashke djevushkoy!" says the young Russian soldier at the entrance to the station demanding my documents. He points

58

to his watches, showing me the time: "Ty neponjemaysh skoljko zcasov? Kuda ty dumaysh poyechatj?" He raises his voice while checking my ID that I am handling to him on his request. "I have to go home", I lie in Russian to his question of where I think I am going, giving him a nice smile and continuing in my school Russian: "I am sorry to be late, comrade, please excuse me". "Mozhesh poyti devushkoy", he returns my smile and let me proceed. The train station looks different from the last time I saw it. Nobody lines up at the ticket counter like there are no travelers. The dirty tile floor of the train hall is covered by thick green military blankets with mostly sleeping Russian soldiers with their Kalishnikov AK-47 next to them. Those of them that are not sleeping yet are rolling cigarettes or are already smoking them. "Zdravstvuj krasavitsa, pochodje syuda, chtoby pokazat sebya!" One of the smoking men attempts to flirt and asks me to come closer so he can see me better. Big bad wolf, I think and avoid getting any closer to him. Others make obscene gestures and laugh. I am embarrassed and disgusted by them. It is not like the times someone is gazing at you in a crowded tram. The heavy cloud of the male odor mixed with cigarette smoke makes me sick to my stomach. The ticket booth is closed, no way to get the ticket. I think I will buy it on the train and keep walking as fast as I can between and across the many sleeping soldiers, avoiding the awakened ones whose stretched arms are trying to reach the parts of my legs that my miniskirt fails to cover. Zombies! I shake off my fear of them.

Finally, I enter the dark unlit underground passage towards the train platforms. Now I am really scared moving through the completely dark passage and begin to shake a bit. The fear is creeping in more and more but I am walking forward. What if some of them followed me here or are waiting for me in the dark? I keep walking fast, turning my head back and forth and side to side, trying to see through the darkness if there is someone there.

Should I rather go back? How safe it would be to go through those bodies again? And where would I go from there? I put together my remaining strength and it overrides my fear. I decide to run through the empty spooky tunnel towards the faint light I can see on its end. I keep running; it is not too far. The dim light is spreading from the platform number 17, the third from the end of the tunnel passage and the only one that seems open. I run towards it; reaching the entry, I climb the stairs leading up to the station. The outdated massive steam locomotive waits on the railroad tracks of the dim platform, puffing clouds of smoke. Only three wagons are connected to it, one of them is a caboose, a post office wagon. Is this a ghost train? Too real for ghosts, but I could imagine those zombies coming out of it any minute now. Get yourself together, I say to myself, there may be nothing safer these days than a ghost train and you already went through those zombies in the hall. Today, real people are still more frightening and even in the day time. I end my silent monologue and choose the middle wagon to enter through its opened door. Just like the outside, there is no one in; it is completely empty, no conductor or ticket clerk. I may even get a free ride. End of the fear. I enter one of the passenger compartments, close its glass door, lock it and spread its dusty curtain over it. Then, I fix myself on the upholstered, not so clean bench by the window. I may be able to sleep all the way through my ride I think, stretching my legs across the seats, using my small duffle bag as a head support. The last, I retrieve my small pocket knife from my purse and hold it opened in the right hand, inside the pocket of my new winter jacket mom stitched for me, now used as a blanket. It takes a while before the train whistle blows loudly and the locomotive puffs a cloud of white steam out of the side of its massive body. Like a thick fog, it covers the platform and my window. I am trying to pierce through the milky whiteness to detect at least a shadow of the station master who blew the whistle. I see nothing except the expelled smoke from the locomotive chimney creeping on the side of the train. With a creaking sound of the wheels moving on the rails, the train begins to move slowly out of the empty station. I feel like a protagonist in the Oriental Express movie and just hope that Hercule Poirot will not have to come to my rescue or, God forbid, solving my murder.

Still before the sunrise, it is dark and cold in the small train station in the outskirts of Budejovice. Not a single soldier is here to stop me to check my ID. I feel unusually free walking in the early morning darkness through the passageway formed by the row of mature linden trees which leaves are symbols of the Czech nation. At this time, I see not a single leaf left on these gentle giants as I see no hope for the Czechs to reverse the misery of the present time.

I walk towards the town and reach its center without problem. On the large square flanked by vaults of the Renaissance houses is a hotel built in an Art Deco style whose name Bell was renamed by the communist regime to Hotel Lenin. I check in at the hotel desk and walk to its breakfast room. Just like the hallway of the hotel, it is empty, but the tables are set for a crowd of travelers, the habit going back to the pre-occupation time. Who are they waiting for now? Served on expensive porcelain there are fresh rolls and pastries accompanied by butter and jams. Small pitchers with cream and large pots of a freshly brewed coffee are ready to be served. I choose a small round table for two and help myself to the most needed breakfast. I start to think my trip to see my love is turning from a horror to a romantic movie.

At 8am I am already standing on the front of the closed gate to the military base. I sign in the visitor book and I wait in the short line of mostly young mothers and their little children and girls of a roughly my age. I see only one older couple with large shopping bags, probably filled with goodies for their loved one. I am bringing nothing to my boyfriend and suddenly feel bad about it. Maybe just my presence here will fix my mistake. But I am starting to get cold waiting in the line exposed to the wind that seems to be bringing with it a freezing rain shower. A handsome soldier, no doubt Czech, walks to the barred fence and calls my name. After assessing my appearance and asking for my ID, he opens the gate for me and leads me across a large courtyard towards some buildings. There are rows of soldiers exercising their marching routines. They obey the commands of their superior officer, looking straight at him. I feel no eye on me. On the far side of the courtyard I see a few old ugly buildings but no Russian soldiers, their tanks or other vehicles. We enter one of the buildings and I wait in an old shabby but sparkling clean hallway for my love to appear. Time runs slow, slower than I would like. Yannek is still not coming. After about an hour and half, another, not so handsome soldier walks directly to me. "Miss", he addresses me in a friendly voice, piercing his gentle eyes through mine, "I am sorry to inform you that private Jaron was transferred this early morning to a military labor camp in an unknown location." He puts his strong fatherly hand on my shoulder and continues: "The private left with me something for you, miss. He said it was very important and will surely cheer you up. I should refrain from private conversations with visitors, but lovely lady, I must say this to you. The man loves you immensely, I am sure of it". At this moment, I am completely catatonic just keep starring into this kind man's eyes. I do not understand and start sobbing and crying, quietly, just on my right eye that I do when things get unbearably cruel. I want to say that I just disobeyed the curfew and walked through hell of Russian occupants just to see my only love, but have no voice to speak. I cannot believe that I am late. "Please, put your coat on", says now firmly the soldier sensing my distress and puts my jacket over my stiff shoulders. "I will escort you out", he continues, inserting the sealed envelope into my hand. Without saying good bye, he releases me back to my world behind the wall of the military base.

With the freezing wind and dark sky, I would have expected snowing but it begins to rain hard as I am walking away without exactly knowing where. The cold rain drenches my face already beaten by the increasingly harsh blows of the wind. Now, I can cry as much as I want and nobody will notice. I am getting soaked and so the envelope still in my hand. I put it in the pocket unopened and walk with my head down against the cruel weather. I am crying into it and with it strolling mindlessly towards a bus stop surrounded by a fast forming puddle of water. I step angrily straight into it splashing the muddy water over my boots, legs, skirt and jacket. I do not care, Yannek is gone.

It is raining heavily now. The large cold raindrops are hitting my knees and thighs exposed by my short skirt. I keep walking away from the bus station towards the town. The nasty rain pierces through my lashes into my eyes and washes my tears off my face with smudges of the makeup. The wind has no mercy on me either, blowing towards me and through me. I am soaking wet and freezing, now looking for a shelter to hide in. Finally, an open church offers me a peaceful hideaway from my misery. I sit down on the wide church pew in the back isle. Only here in the safety of the sacred space, I open the wet envelope from Yannek. There is a letter for me and a hundred crown bill. I do not understand the money until I finish reading the long love letter. It is a sweet letter, revealing Yannek's love for me but somehow I feel shocked by its rather forceful ending: *I am choosing you. I love you forever and will marry you. Wait for me until I come back. I will be earning a little money and will always send it to you. Do not spend it, save it! When I come back we should have enough for our wedding rings. From now on, you have to wait for me. Be faithful to me. Consider yourself being engaged to me. Love is eternal. Your fiancé Yannek.*

I am looking in disbelief into the flame of the candle next to the altar. It is hypnotizing, but I am firmly in my own thoughts. Yannek is my first and true love and I do not want to change him for anyone. I love him and miss him greatly but what is this assumption of us being engaged without my consent? What rights does my boyfriend have to tell me what I should consider without asking me if I want to? I try to make some sense of it. He must feel lonely and hurt by the alienation he suffers through the judgment and punishment he disagrees with. He meant well for the country, thinking that his opinion and judgment was better than the officer's order and therefore should have been considered. He was patriotic and did not want to succumb to the occupants without a fight. But he gave orders that he was not entitled to do. Is he doing the same to me now? He wants me to obey his order, without looking at my side of the thing. I am choosing you. Consider yourself being engaged to me, he says, what a way to ask for marriage. It feels like a verbal rape. I do not want my sweetheart to be an executioner of my will. I do not want him to tell me to obey him. If I wanted to share my life with him, I would like to make my choices as he would his. I am unable to act positively upon Yannek's wish that dictates me to blindly follow, to be obedient to him. It would be the same as following orders just for the sake of some ideology or fear of authority. I need to decide on my own, I need to be considered. I take the hundred crown bill from the envelope and stuff it into one of the donation boxes by the altar.

I light a small candle and put it under the picture of Mary. It is for Yannek to wish him well. It is for those jailed unjustly, as well as the others that will be. It is for love and respect. It is for all women, who like me, need to speak for selves, not to be spoken for. I stare at the man nailed to the cross, the seeker of love and truth in the face of power and violence. I look at the contorted tortured man and begin to feel his pain as if it was my own. I too want someone to feel my suffering. I am also a searcher of love and truth and I fight against the imposition of power on will. Would anyone understand? I think, no one can.

I still look like I am crying when I walk out of the church into the rain. But I am not. It is just my broken heart sobbing for the loss of my first love.

EXISTENCE

I am exiting a local train at Zbuch, a little mining town where I
live in the school dormitory. It is exactly 3:24 pm and a crowd of
young people sets for a one mile and half walk to the dorm. It is
already getting dark; snowflakes are falling from the sky, settling
gently on my hair and lashes and my new jacket my mom stitched
for me. It feels like the day in Prague when I first met Daniel. It is

peaceful, so peaceful.

The young Russian soldier that was left behind by his troops no longer stands here. My friend is telling me that he was not allowed to leave his post where he was waiting for his comrades to return to him. They left him behind. Without fresh water, food and help he got very sick and eventually died on starvation and dehydration. On Saturday, the local coal miners are going to have a hockey match with the Russian soldiers now stationed in Zbuch barracks. I wonder who will win this time.

It is snowing densely now. The wet sticky snowflake clusters drift in the wind, attaching selves everywhere. The houses by the slippery road we are walking on are turning white. And it keeps snowing. I will make a little snowman by the front door to the dorm, I think happily. It will be like in the good old days of my happy childhood. Already from the distance, I can see there is a lot of commotion on the front of the gym next to my dorm. As I come closer, I spot an ambulance parked in the driveway. The wind blows the white snow on its front windows, settling at their corners. My friends are standing next to it motionless. They are waiting for something or someone in a strange morbid silence. The snow falls on their hair and shoulders and accumulates on them as they stand there like lifeless statues. The sorrowful face grimaces are complemented by the slowly melting snow dripping down across their cheeks. A stretcher with a black bag is being taken from the building to the ambulance. Snowflakes fall on its shiny plastic making small white spots on it that turn almost instantly into tiny water puddles. It confuses me; I do not understand what is going on. The whiteness of the air and the ground makes this place look surreal. Everything around seems to stop in the quietness of the moment. It feels like any minute all will assent to heaven. It is like the white feather is falling down from angels' wings on our catatonic selves. Is this a message of sorrow or love? Someone interferes in the silence with a tantrum that breaks into my personal enlightenment. "Why, why?" my friend Nelly shouts. I am learning that Anthony is dead. He hanged himself this early morning on the basketball hoop. He was waiting for Nelly to return to him and bring back love to their broken relationship. She was not coming but he kept waiting until he could not any longer. I recall the dead Russian soldier of about the same age. He was also waiting. Everybody today is waiting for something, often not knowing for what.

At my dorm I was handled two letters today. My mom writes from Prague. Last night, my brother was shot in the leg by a Soviet soldier while posting some anti-occupant pamphlets on the City Hall. He is OK though, she writes, he managed to escape through the nearby parks. He got home with quite a loss of blood. What a soldier, writes mom. I always think these days about war and all those terrible things that make people to become soldiers, fighters and haters. Are we at war with each other or is it just the state of living and the need for survival in this cruel gray world? The letter number two is from Daniel.

Dear Adella, I am sitting by the window at one of the small round tables in the Café Slavia, writing a letter to you. I can see that across the street at the National Theater there is a quite a crowd of people but more police and Russian soldiers, must be a big deal. I think, they are about to arrest someone from the theater, someone well known who speaks openly and loudly against the occupation and regime. I hope it is not Triska, a great actor and a brave one too. It is pretty lousy here in Prague, you may be better off where you are. The Czechoslovak TV is also undergoing a large political reform to embrace the Russian prescription of totality. Every day of my job now, I swallow my words and I zip my mouth most of the time. Soon, I may become completely catatonic. The security guards at work are the Big Brothers' ears and tell on everyone who says something against the regime. I really want to see you, Adella, you struck me hard. I think I am beginning to fall in love. See you soon, Yours, Danny.

He may be in love, but I do not think I am. Still, I feel close to Daniel. Maybe there could be some hope found in life with him. It is not all too rational but there is some strange feeling in me to jump into this relationship as long as it continues to move somewhere, anywhere where I was not before. Despite of the fact that such a relationship may not even work, I am stepping into it. At this time, when we live in the shadow of the occupation and autocratic government disallowing basic human rights, I am taking my chance to live, to enjoy a ride away from all of this. I need some peace of mind and hope that it is my personal freedom that will bring me happiness. I put the letters under the pillow of my top bank bed and walk towards the window. It is snowing peace out there.

WILHELM

I know I am thinking too much but I cannot help myself. I know that some rebellions still remain, but a pen has replaced the sword. The 'normalization process' that has followed the occupation is just a vicious hunt for those who continue to write the truth. Writers and intellectuals are disappearing from the public sight. Some of those, who managed to leave the country during the short period of opened borders before the occupation, now write in exile. Here, the strong repression of human rights attempts to create a systemic obedience. People now live in a kind of vacuum existence. It is a very slow, dull, grey living. I guess that is why I have gotten together with much older Daniel. He is my safety. The weekends spent in the green countryside bring a little more smile to my face. Movies, books, arts and friendships take me away from thinking about the sad destiny that creeps at all levels of our lives. My life is turning into a dependence on friends and parties. I know it is just the opposite of my true desire to be independent rather than marching in line with those who exchanged their social liberty for a personal one. But at the same time, I still rebel against it and I test myself through the deep friendship with Wilhelm. It is the only piece of independence I have left. The tram is full today as ever; it is 7:45 am. At eight, I have to open our electronic shop and get ready for customers. My job is not bad and I enjoy it even though my working days are pretty long, from eight to six. But I have two hours long lunch breaks and they are the best part of my day. It is not at all about the food or the break from the work monotony that I enjoy so much, but the free spirited time I spend with Wilhelm. I am enchanted by him, his tall, slim, gentle looks and intelligent demeanor. I make myself believing that one day we will marry. His kissing makes me feel that way. But when we walk together in the streets of Prague, we look more like siblings than lovers. My long blond hair is neatly brushed reaching the middle of my back, his beautiful silky ones are bumping up and down on his shoulders as he walks, like he was some marionette prince. My current boyfriend has nothing of him. I think I love Wilhelm. Oh, the tram stops and I am getting out and rushing to open the shop. It is pretty cold here.

The slowly disappearing winter is leaving behind puddles of dirty melting snow. The city of Prague is gloomy under the dark cloudy sky. It is my lunch break. Today, Wilhelm and I are taking a long walk to a restaurant for lunch. We are silent, just occasionally looking at each other and holding hands like lowers do. I am wishing that we kiss again, like we did yesterday, in the open on the crowded street. It was thrilling, adrenaline rushing, like doing something that is not allowed. As we were making out, I kept looking into his eyes as if it was a vast universe. I saw cosmic dust coming from this universe and settling slowly on my lashes and face. The reality of the moment was suspended indefinitely in my mind.

We reached the restaurant hidden in the corner of the Lesser Town Square. The food was good and cheap and we are now walking back along the shore of the river Vltava. It is beautiful, still partially frozen; floating pieces of broken ice bounce at each other slightly and swoop in the river current out of the view. We are kissing a bit clumsily today. I am on my toes, Wilhelm with his head lowered to a side. I am pretty excited but the expected cosmic miracle does not happen today. It is just kissing, nothing else. Still, my cheeks are getting hot and nervousness begins to spreads from my mind to my body. My brain just does not let me relax. I keep my eyes closed and start to feel the vertigo of the Earth turning. I know we are soul mates and belong together; there is so much of ease in our passionate spontaneous ways. Our view of the world, politics and our cultural interests connect us beautifully. We admire each other's strength. I believe, together we could fight for our ideals against anybody. Breaking our loving embrace, Wilhelm takes my hand and leads me towards an old deserted bench in the children's playground. We sit down close to each other, but I lose my patience and get up abruptly. I am stricken by sudden sadness as I look at the empty little barge that is rocking slowly in the river current.

The reality tells me that Wilhelm and I will never be together, he is not my boyfriend and he is not my love. Just face it, I said to myself: We are only friends, each of us more in love with one's rebellious self than the other. We interact without promises and obligations. We walk on the sidelines of our lives; our relationship and closeness have no rules and no guidance. To us, it is the missing freedom that we create together. When we are in the lover's embrace, the whole world turns around 360 degrees and becomes only ours. In our world, we do not need to rebel against the reality that dictates us its orders. We are no longer objects of the society dictatorship that treats us like some books ready to be catalogued and stacked on the library shelves. We both know, but are not brave to say it aloud: We cannot get closer than that, we need our alternate reality away from the world we live in. This is our rebellion against the world that is not free. That lack of freedom is the missing puzzle in our relationship. Wilhelm will always be the escape from reality for me, the shelter to hide from harm, the laughter found in the time of despair, the friend whom I will always love.

It is close to my wedding to Daniel. Wilhelm invites me time to time to join him for coffee, a bottle of wine or a theater performance, but we are not the same. Most days, after I close the shop, we leave separately to our own destinations, to our own personal reality without even looking at each other. My wedding to Daniel is going to happen and I know it will be impossible to continue my relationship with Wilhelm after that. Everything has to be changed. I will be exchanging my miniskirt for a maxi wedding dress. I have to grow up into a lady worthy of the wedding in the majestic castle near Prague. For Daniel, it rings a noble beginning to our new life. To me, the castle wedding is an illusionary shelter from the communist reality and a kind of dive back in time into the medieval fantasy. But my life after that will be different. I will become a wife, living in a lovely suburban villa. I am barely twenty years old and I will be stabilized, no more rebellions or protesting in the streets of Prague, no more opposing the government or my man's rules. I will be normalized like the rest of the country. I will fit into my life. How about love? Will it find its way to us? Some say that what love really is, the warmth and light for the other. If it is so, my heart must surely be from elsewhere, because to me, love, like the sun, is not just a source of warmth and light but a burning element and the essence of life. Will it find its way to us?

Wilhelm and I are completely apart now. I miss him. He works in a different location, far away from our shop and I work with a new company. We have not seen each other for many years. Our estrangement is now final and our lives continue in separate ways. It had been hard on me, my soul had been crying for him incessantly for a long time but it is silent now. Just the memories have remained.

More time has passed. We have been living in the most oppressive political epoch since the communist turnover after the Second World War. Many activist and leaders pursuing democratic change have been arrested, amongst them one of the creator of Charta 77, Vaclav Havel. My life also has taken a surprising turn, politically and personally and it is giving me no choice but to emigrate from my country, somewhere to safety, somewhere I will start over again.

I am saying goodbyes to my family and the people close to me, pretending a short vacation. I know I need to find Wilhelm before I depart, it has been years since we had last seen each other. I am finding him in one of the Prague's electronic service shops. Wilhelm's silky hair is beginning to thin down a bit, but his eyes and smile are the same, gently boyish. He is married with a child. We are talking a little, but our spontaneity we once had is gone. A bit of melancholy strikes me when I see that Wilhelm found his happiness without me. My marriage is over and I am going to look for my contentment elsewhere not knowing if I will ever find it. We are saying the last goodbye, the hugs and kisses are missing; there is barely any eye contact between us as if we are both guilty of some strange betrayal. I am giving him my favored book, perhaps because I just want to give him something to remember me by. It is The Gulag Archipelago written by Aleksandr Solzhenitsyn, the book that is still banned to distribute in our country. There is nothing else I can give him; I no longer owe anything in this country and I am leaving everything and my whole life behind. I know that my escape is definite; there is no way out of it. Yet, I wish I could stay because this farewell falls on me like a heavy stone. I am devastatingly sad but keeping my tears in. It is only now that I sense deeply that Wilhelm and I have never been just friends, there had been a deeper connection between us. But as I did before, I am leaving him again, only this time I have no choice. Still, guilt is creeping in as it had happened at the time of my wedding when I had abandoned Wilhelm for Daniel. Our last greeting goes, as always, only a half way, unfinished. My soul keeps protesting against its torture, some silly loving feeling is radiating out of it. What does this late love has to do with it, it is all in vain.

We stand close to each other for a long time silently, and then finally hug and kiss. It is the last hug with the friendly little kisses on the cheeks. Sometime ago we belonged to each other. We had never made love; our relationship was pure and platonic. It was an extraordinary love, the kind one always remembers. But I know today that we will never see each other again.

PART THREE

Reconstruction of Memory

LIKE A SNOWFLAKE

She was born in Prague five minutes before midnight on the Summer Solstice Day. The whole city was in bloom that day and so she got her middle name Blossom after the blooming city to always remember that. Her surname, however, was Vera, the name derived from veritas, meaning truth. But there are two sides of the coin to the story. The night of her birth a snow flurry began to fall on the roofs of the ancient city. The snowflakes slowly accumulated into a thin layer of snow and covered the blooming city lightly, giving it a special spark. When the story of her birth was later reveled to her, she secretly wished her name was Snowflake, so she would carry the memory of that magic summer solstice event.

My life in the communist society I was born into went along with the thirteen millions of others that frowned every day over their gray existence and hoped that someday everything will change if not to be great to be at least better. The major break in that monotonous life happened with the so called Prague Spring 1968, a political reform that forcefully ended by Soviet occupation of the country. Almost ten years later, a written demand to the government called Charta 77 brought hopes for another change. This important pamphlet, created by an intellectual and political movement, asked the totalitarian government to guarantee the people freedom of speech, rights to assemble, free press and other liberties that were denied to them. Since I was already involved in the distribution of censored dissident press, I began dispersing to the public this important document as well. But at the end of the same year 1977, the government secret police started to watch me. My apartment and even my garbage were searched multiple times when I was at work. I slowed down my activist efforts a bit, but still continued to help in hope that all will end well for our democracy. It felt it was worthy. The freedom seemed to be waiting just around the corner. Was it really?

Is it worth fighting for truth? I am asking myself now. I know it was, it always is, but now I am scared. I am sitting here in the police station, petrified what is going to happen to me. Two men are about to interrogate me. I am holding tight my small shopping bag as if it is my treasure and safety. I feel dizzy in my head and barely understand how I got here. I was returning from the supermarket, that I know, when these two secret police agents stopped me, shoved me in their car and drove me to this police establishment known as a notorious torture prison. They are not questioning me yet, it is just intimidation. One of them rips my shopping bag from my hand and kicks it away to the corner of the room. The broken eggs start to leak out; I am surprised the empty glass bottle from milk did not break. There was no milk or bread to buy today, so eggs is all I got. "Are you working against the government? Are you distributing illegal anti-government materials? ", one of the men starts now the interrogation very loudly. "I was shopping." I said. They are asking more and more questions but I feel far away, I do not understand. They are getting angry and I am really afraid. I say nothing. They ask about some names I have never heard of. I am so stressed, becoming completely catatonic. Now, they are covering my head with a heavy green something that is itchy. It is probably a heavy military blanket. They hold it tight around my face; it does not let me breathe properly. They do this head wrap between questioning me about something. I do not properly hear the questions. The blanket is now wrapped over my head tightly and they hold my arms behind my back. I am terrified, struggling to breathe and only wishing hard that I do not die here. I cannot cry, my eyes are shut; I am choking now, my throat aches, my chest is tight...I struggle somehow, trying to move my head and arms. I want to shake that thing of my shoulders and pull my arms from the hold, but nothing works. I want to scream, I want to cry – I cannot. I cannot. I shake inside and feel numbed all over. I struggle again in vain and panic. They let go; I am catching my breath, coughing and get a nose bleed. My body is shaking in a shock. They are laughing at me. "Here is some water for you, bitch!" one of them shouts and gives me mercifully a half empty glass of water. "And get the fuck out of here you trash, you skinny fucking slut!" They are kicking me out of the room into a tiled hallway towards the exit. I do not care about their insults and their harsh treatment.

They are letting me go! Oh God, thank you, life is great! Life is so great, great, great, great, I sing in my head when the station gate closes after me.

From now on, I know that they keep watching my every move, wherever I go. I see them. There are like ghosts invading my privacy. I am grateful for my life but it is a scary one. My existence shatters and my worries about being taken back for a torturous interrogation or to be persuaded to collaborate are pretty real. All my social and political connection had to be disconnected. I am also learning that some of my colleagues, who like me, were involved in the banned press distribution, were arrested or emigrated to the West. I too may have to escape abroad to avoid my imprisonment. I am thinking of it more and more, but have no one to talk to about it. It is always in my head, I trust no one, but want to tell somebody or want to get close to someone to feel safer. Would loving someone give me more strength to overcome this dreadful existence? How about the rape attempt by my former friend Karl? How could I forget? How much more of these rapes if political or sexual I can handle? The devastation from these experiences is profound, yet it helps me to understand how far the unwanted political power went. It affects the way of life, ethics and politics and gives licenses to the powerful to demand, to rape or imprison anyone they decide to: the innocent and the powerless, the ones who oppose or simply the ones who spread the truth.

I keep bringing back these memories of the past, especially today. It was on April 4th, 1978 when I left my home in Prague on the pretext of traveling on a short vacation but managed to immigrate to Vienna, Austria. The communist permit to travel had to be falsified, because under the circumstances, I would not be able to get a real one. And I was supposed to return in four days…thankfully I did not. I knew I would never be able to come back unless the country's politics changed. I had a good friend, a companion with whom I drove across the border, but each of us, on the end, went our own way. It has not been easy to start again, alone, to start everything anew. My life went on hold for some time without my slight knowledge of how would I manage to survive in a foreign country whose language I did not know. Yet, the crossing of the border to Austria made me already understand that the day of my escape was an apex of my life. It was as thrilling as it was frightening. It felt like mountain climbing without belaying, knowing one has to reach the peak but may also fall to one's death. The vagina search on the Czech side of the boarder was awful and unacceptable but I said to myself: as humiliating and abusive this is I will prevail. The last rape, I called it, no more. Allowed to cross to the other side, I sensed my victory. I was free. It felt like a new beginning, like I was born again. That day on April 4, 1978, I had crossed the border between Czechoslovakia and Austria; it was about 4:30 pm.

My child was born today, ten years later here in the United States, in the City of Brotherly Love. I went to labor in about 2 pm, the same time I had arrived, ten years ago, to the border crossing towards my freedom. It feels extraordinary. Just like me at that time, after the hardship to free self, my baby as well, took the first long breath of freedom at about 4:30 pm. Born in the USA, under the Bill of Rights of the United States of America, his freedom is from now on guaranteed to him as his inalienable right. For me, this freedom had to be searched for, fought for; my freedom had to be found.

Exhausted after the birth and with her recollections, Vera turns her head towards the window in her birthing room. A large crown of a flowering tree dominates the view. The blossoms are delicate lightly pink, freshly open and very attractive. She cannot get her eyes off them when, all of a sudden, gently, like white feathers of angels, snow flurries begin to settle on the blooming crown of the tree. The snowflakes are gliding one by one in the air, landing quietly in all their majesty, each a different design, on the tree and glass window of her room: Magic on the day her child was born. It is snowing in April. She recalls the story of her own birth and smiles. Is it some biological mimicry or merely coincidence? It seems like a reflection of the past, this snowing out of season. She recognizes the affinities between her past and her present. The memory trace of her difficult border crossing to freedom came to her again and activates the past strong emotions. Like her that day, crossing the line to freedom, her newborn struggled today out of the womb to live. It feels like her life recycled itself into something new, something even more beautiful. Perhaps our lives run in cycles of similarities. Some people's life experiences may closely resemble each other; some become almost a reflection of another. Our life stories may intertwine with others' and our struggles and desires may lead us to the same or a similar path. Common grounds, but we are not the same. Like snowflakes we are born in our vast magical universe to be recognized through

our uniqueness in a never-ending cycle of life.

VELVET REVOLUTION

It was that gloomy dark day in cold November 17, 1989 in Prague when the unexpected happened. The nation of the powerless united against the Power Giant in the search for dignity, human rights, liberty and democracy. The "power of the powerless" of Vaclav Havel's description of the totalitarian state had gained that day a different meaning.

"Oh no, another defeat", frowns exhausted Patrick after being miraculously saved from his arrest by crawling under the parked police car to his safety. As he passes the statue of St. Wenceslas on now the empty square, he recalls a daisy, a symbol of peace, one of the student demonstrators gave to him. He gets out the dying daisy from his jeans pocket and puts it at the foot of the statue. Standing there in silence with his eyes closed he thinks away from this unhappy world. Alternate reality is what we need. We used to create one with my best friend. Was it to forget the world or to armor ourselves against life assaults? It is all gone now; we were brave as knights those days but did not keep the hope. Is it just our defeat we people suffer today or is it the despair and disdain for the future? Czech legend about Blanik Knights comes to his mind. I wish it was the truth, not just the other world reality, he thinks. The knights are waiting inside the cave in the legendary Mountain Blanik for the right time to act on the behalf of the country. Such time would come when the nation's suffering becomes unbearable. The knights would exit the mountain's cave and ride against the enemy which they would defeat in a victorious battle leaving the nation in peace and prosper for at least one hundred years. Patrick sighs: Such a dreadful day, a terrible defeat and it is my birthday. He raises his head towards the equestrian statue of St. Wenceslas. He feels like a little boy looking up towards the majestic equestrian statue and he whispers: "The only thing I wish for my birthday is the help of the Blanik Knights. Please help us; we cannot carry any longer our burden alone. I wish you could arise and bring back our peace and democracy". He stands peacefully before the monument for a long time before he turns around walks away, looking in dismay on the empty square. The abandoned battlefield still carries the signs of the police assaults. Perhaps soon, he thinks, the snow will fall and all the prints of pain will be buried under it and forgotten, but the hurt will be buried inside us, the hurt will stay.

The black & white movie that had shown those days after the November 17, 1989 in every cinema, every school and every possible public space was actually an official police video. It recorded the police actions against the citizens on that November 1989. The official documentary was leaked to the Czechoslovak Press by the two police filmmakers themselves:

November 17, 1989, Wenceslas Square, Prague

Transcript

A young father carries a child in his arms: "Do not let them to beat us, please, please, people. Do not let them to beat us. Help, help!" pleads another man running away from a policeman that follows him. A couple, visibly beaten, tries to inspire others not to let go: "We cannot let it go this way!" they shout loud before the man gets a hard kick in the crotch from the policeman wearing heavy boots. He falls down, squealing in pain. An anti-riot clad policeman stands above him with his baton out: "Stop pretending" he yells at the man under him, "nothing happened to you!" Another police trooper approaches a photographer and rips of the camera hanging on his neck. "Not my camera!" the photographer manages to scream in despair but the camera already flies in the air. He tries to catch it but the policeman hits his calf hard with the baton. The man falls to his knees with a visible grimace of pain on his face. He cries loud in confusion: "They broke my camera! I have rights to record this! Where is our freedom of press? "You have what? Where is your what? You did not have enough?" asks the policeman in anger and begins to hit the photographer's back with his baton. A line of riot police with dogs is being formed opposite the crowd. The German Shepherds are excited and bark loudly. "Let's go boys, let's get them!" the officers command their dogs. The men and the dogs run aggressively against the people on front of them who are not in any kind of organized group, merely standing on the front of the monumental statue of St. Wenceslas, the legendary king of the nation. The dog squad is getting close to an old woman. She tries to walk away from them as fast as she can but slips and falls onto the sidewalk. The woman puts her face close to the ground to avoid a dog bite: "Don't touch me" she manages to call courageously. On the opposite sidewalk a man is carrying a large painted canvas that have a tear in the middle. "My work is broken", says he sadly, "They did it. I was just going home." "People, keep recording what the pigs are doing! ", says loudly a young reporter with a movie camera "But watch out, they are confiscating films and cameras", she adds and gets to work, recording all the happenings. A middle aged woman walks with her teenage children. They move swiftly on the sidewalk away from the demonstrators. Two policemen halt them and without any further questions or examination start poking them with the batons. The mother steps on the front of the children and pushes the brutes away. "You are touching an official, get your hands off or you will be arrested", shouts loudly to her face a riot squad policeman. "Get away from my children", she replies in a loud protective voice. The police finally let them go. A young man in his twenties is lying in a fetal position on the sidewalk and sighs in pain. His older father tries to protect his body from the fast approaching police with dogs. He cries for help: "My son is recovering from a spinal surgery and they knocked him down, please help us people, he cannot get up and they will run over him."

An army vehicle with large automatic weapons is nearing. "They are enclosing student demonstrators on National Avenue" says loudly a young student with a bouquet of daisies in her arm. She continues to run to the direction of that avenue past the vehicle mounted with a machine gun and offers her daisies to the policemen on the vehicle, signing a peace to them. They ignore her. A military transport with water cannon enters from the side street. A small group of people sits on the corner of the sidewalk, some hold flowers in their hands. They are singing the national anthem: "Where is my home, where is my home…"An amplified voice overwhelms the sound of the song: "Citizens give up you efforts or we will use force against you." the voice keeps repeating. Here and there, people are crying, flowers are being stepped on, sound of pain is heard somewhere in the distance but there is no fear on the peoples' faces anymore. "We will not surrender! We will not surrender!" shout voices from the crowd. "We will persist, freedom is near!" a group of student keeps repeating in a loud unison from the top of the St. Wenceslas statue that they climbed on. They are setting Czech flag next to the king's one. Crowd repeats their slogan. "We will persist, freedom is near!"A policeman looks and walks in the direction that the slogans are coming from, but the people continue repetitively: "No violence! We have enough of repression! Pigs go home! We want new government!" Fascists, fascists, fascist!" calls a man standing upright on a garbage can with his both arms stretched towards the sky as if calling the heavens for justice. A police officer kicks and pushes down the garbage can he stands on. The man is falling down on his face still with his arms stretched up. Somewhere, people are starting to sing the national anthem again. More police with dogs runs against the newly formed crowd. All of a sudden, a tall old bearded man with a long grey hair dressed like an ancient priest raises his head and shoulders magically up from the crowd as if elevated by some sacred powers. Visibly above the crowd in silence, the priest faces prophetically his enemy. He says nothing, just stands there proudly and peacefully in his passive resistance. A dog gets close to him and jumps high on his chest, pushing him down. "That's him, here he is, we got him!" rejoices a policeman's voice. "Arrest him, comrade", commands an officer in charge pointing to the old priest who is now falling down to the ground backwards slowly with his legs raised up and moving slightly in the air. A powerful stream of water comes from the water cannons on the trucks parked directly against the protesters. People disperse and run away if they can. Some of them are falling down under the high pressure stream of water from the cannon. The gathering here is defeated, but many protesters unite again, now marching towards the National Avenue, south of the square. There they are met with the large group of students coming from the Faculty of Charles University. But the police force is ready for them, waiting. Once the two groups join together, a convoy of heavy transporters equipped with front shovels surrounds the demonstrators from all sides. These bulldozer like vehicles drive towards the people to make them to back up to the wall where there is no way to escape. The large crowd of demonstrators is pressed together tightly and people begin to step and fall over each other. Some are trapped underneath and stepped on. They gasp for air and space. Huge panic and loud screams and cries make this situation a horror site. A few people from the side of the crowded mass manage to crawl and hide under the vehicles parked by the sidewalk. Police starts to pull them out and beat them. A special force squad drags all captured protestors away to the prepared fenced enclosures similar to those used in the fields for controlling sheep. There they are being beaten before their arrest. The injured individuals are taken into police vans and driven away. Others are driven away in large military trucks. Eventually, the street is clear of people, but the police force and the vehicles stay.

Some defeats are important steps towards victory. Not surprisingly, the so called Velvet Revolution remembered as a clash between students and police, also recalled its early physical defeats on the streets of Prague in the days before and on November 17, 1989. But the brutality of the police did not stop the resistance that was an important step towards the long waiting change towards democracy. During that year and after, the nation united under the new leadership of Vaclav Havel, the playwright and dissident, one of the contributors of the human rights pamphlet Charta 77. A new temporary government and democratic constitution was formed. Then, in the free election of 1990, Vaclav Havel was voted the first president of the newly created democratic Czechoslovakia.

BACK TO THE START

I am visiting my birth town. It is late autumn, twenty five years after the Velvet Revolution that established freedom and democracy in now Czech Republic. It is cold, the sky is dark; it may snow or rain any minute. I am standing in a crowd of people in the first courtyard of the Prague Castle waiting for the arrival of the president of the Czech Republic. As the others, I am curious what the president has to say to the people. He is not popular with many. I notice a tall well built middle aged man standing at the edge of the waiting crowd. His face is directed towards the baroque gateway from which the presidential group shall enter the castle courtyard. The gate is guarded by two theatrically clad soldiers whose function is to impress the tourists rather than to actually safeguard the gates. It is a charming picture, straight from a fairy tale. Other, more serious police officers in black combat outfits guard the road from where the presidential cars should arrive.

The president, his body guards, his speaker and the media are finally on the site. The tall man I have noticed before made himself to stick out above the crowd. He is standing on a wooden box. As the president turns towards the waiting crowd, the man on the box, like some historical speaker for democracy in the British Hyde Park, addresses the president loudly: "Mr. President!

Respectfully, Mr. President" he is shouting loud to be heard: "Greetings!" He seems to get the president's attention for a moment and a crowd of photographers points their cameras towards him. Quickly, he takes his sweat shirt off and slowly turns around on his box. His now exposed back and chest show slogans written in black on it. It reads: WE DO NOT LIKE YOUR POLITICS! WE WANT HAVEL'S DEMOCRACY BACK! WE WANT YOUR RESIGNATION! Not everything is possible to read from my position in the crowd. But I can see that the man is peaceful, just turning around in silence showing the writings on his body. Freedom of expression; I am glad to see it and smile a little. But all of a sudden three police officers rush towards the man, kicking the box under him and knocking him to the ground. I am outraged, recalling a news footage from Prague Velvet Revolution crushes of 1989: a heroic looking man standing on the garbage can. He as well was knocked down to the ground for exercising his freedom of expression. As I am coming closer to the area where the man is, I can see that he is being handcuffed and arrested without his rights being stated to him. One of the policemen kicks slightly his behind with his knee and slaps him over the naked back even though the man is totally submitting to him. I cannot believe this. "What did this man do to arrest him and use brutality?" I ask, but get no answer. "He has rights to his freedom of speech and expression", says a standing by citizen. We both begin again to question the police behavior. "Your questions will be answered in tonight police news", answers a policewoman watching the people who are now watching the police. "Step away. No one comes closer. Back up, there is a police line here, anyone crossing over may be arrested," she continues. People back up and stop paying attention to the happening. The man is taken into a police car. He is still bare-chested with a grin on his face and walks with his captors proudly towards their car. With the writing of freedom on his body he looks like a tattooed Celtic warrior captured by Roman soldiers. I smile at him and show a peace sign. He winks his eye. He will keep testing his rights in democracy and he will fight injustice. I am sure of it and admire his ways. We are never alone in this world looking for our freedom. The president is waving to the tourists, the Prague citizens are not here – not today, maybe tomorrow if Vaclav Havel's democracy returns.

The snow begins to fall coloring that beautiful world of Prague with a silvery white paint. I am making my way through the powdery mash downhill on Nerudova Street towards the Charles Bridge that stretches majestically over the Vltava River. The bridge has stayed strong on-guard like some medieval knight since the 14th Century. It is a poetic sight and a location worthy of a romantic movie. Under the heavy arches of the bridge formed by strong pillars, white swans glide gracefully on the silver water fluffing obsessively their feathered tutus for the ballet of their own. The gulls are flying above the bridge with loud cries, catching in the air pieces of bread that people throw to them. Some of them rest their wings on the heads of the statues that flank the ancient bridge. The army of pigeons on the ground is pecking on pieces of bread that the gulls did not catch in the air. I see the Man-God nailed on a giant cross; he has some birds resting on his shoulders and head. It adds a bit of joy and beauty to the scenery of the suffering. A large raven, like a black angel, is flying down from the white snowy heaven above. She lands on the head of the crucified while the angelic pigeons respectfully look up to her from bellow. The spirit of the moment creates a gracious silence that spreads all over this magical place. Peace, love and freedom descend onto the earth with that light white falling snow. Is this all real? This tranquility, on one hand, that seems eternal and on the other hand, the arrogance I have just witnessed not so long ago. I hope the people here will always protect their freedom. I know what lack of freedom means. I lived through it.

I am so glad I am here but the flying to Prague for the first time since my emigration was quite overwhelming. We flew over the White Mountain. I saw the river Vltava and the foggy landscape bellow it, my Mountain of Sisyphus with the red and yellow leaves of October. Traces of snow covered its ground. How much I had loved this mountain, running down and climbing back up again. When I close my eyes thinking of nothing, I can still feel the energy of my beloved river, jumping over the boulders and hissing like a snake in every turn…I had rolled down from my mountain to my river in pain and the river saved me. I had followed its current all the way to the West and across the ocean to a new land. I had changed, my country of birth had changed but the river stayed the same, my Vltava! After all these years of absence here I will have to reconstruct my memory in the face of the new democratic Czech Republic. I am looking forward to my lecture at Charles University and to the meeting with people to discuss their experiences during the Revolution of 1989. It should be pretty rewarding and I can add a report on that to my forthcoming book.

There is still so much on my mind. My life away from here is good. But the appreciation of my work by my academic colleagues is in contrast with my personal life. Those I used to know and love here seem to abandon me. I am only a visitor in this country, but I still care for it. I am a foreigner and yet I am not. Being here feels like going back to the start, back in time.

PATTERN
RECONSTRUCTION

I have been in Prague for over two months now. I buried my

mother's ashes, after spending with her the last days of her life.

Those days with her had helped me to understand death in a more

deep and intimate sense. It is always love that matters, even in

dying; the only fear that is left is not of the leaving the world of reality for something unknown, but the fear of the love leaving us forever. In this way, dying is not that different from living and loving. Throughout my life, I have been looking for love and understanding so I am not left alone in life and death. But I think love will really never leave us. It may live on even after our death by being passed onto the others, from generation to generation as inheritance. It also lives through our memories and past recollections and reveals itself in our actions. It is the love experience that transcends and transforms human existence towards the true love, even at the end of life and maybe beyond. Love may be, indeed, universal.

The snowy mash of yesterday is gone. Prague seems gloomy under the cloudy skies. I keep looking for my soul mate even though I feel I will never find him. I am wondering through Kampa Park, walking on the shores of the river Vltava, sitting on the wet benches in children's playgrounds, wasting time in coffee shops, having lunches in the restaurants we used to go together. I am peeking nostalgically into the winery at the end of Manes Bridge where we had spent a long time ago a happy evening together. I keep searching for the venues we had visited together but they seem not to exist anymore. It is all different here in the twenty five years older Prague. The renovated restaurants offer international foods instead of the Czech ones, Starbucks took over my favored coffee shop, many theaters closed or moved elsewhere. I am also different; it is only my soul that is acting the same as long ago, wanting to connect with the other one of my soul mate. He is surely different person if he is still alive. Everything had changed; only the old river Vltava is the same, moving steadily forward and whispering the same sad melody of the past. I walk close to its bank and sit inside an abandoned little boat tied with a chain to a pole on the shore. It is an old fisherman pram without oars, with a bit of dirty water inside. My heart is pounding as my boat rocks gently on the river tide. How foolish I am looking for Wilhelm. I know I will never see him again and maybe I do not even want to. It is just a game of paradoxes and an unfinished puzzle of my life that is missing just one last piece. After all, I do not even remember his real name.

Out of the river bank and across the bridge, I am passing the corner of Plzenska and Nadrazni Streets near Prague Andel station. There was our electronic shop somewhere over there I go on with that silly game of mine again, testing my memory. A new commercial glass structure replaced the nineteen century building. Beautiful, but an alien structure, runs through my head. And here on the corner, used to be a bakery shop. We were having dates here with Daniel after my work. I give the spot a long nostalgic look. An older couple is meeting there with a friendly on the cheeks kisses. She is elegant and radiant, about the same age as me. He looks like someone I may have seen before. He is tall, much taller than the woman; his thin face with the short beard reminds me a bit of Wilhelm. Old Wilhelm, ha ha, no way, I think, just let it go. I turn my head away from the two of them and walk slowly from the Andel station in the direction of the Café Slavia.

Vera enters the infamous Slavia Café situated across the street from the Prague National Theater. Patrick, the participant of the demonstrations against government police forces during the revolution of 1989, is already waiting to be interviewed by her. He sits at a round table for two near the window. Vera joins him and their conversation picks up. In the back of the café a piano man plays Chopin's Polonaise. "As you know, Patrick, I was referred to you because you are one of the people who had experienced the harshness of the police force during November 1989 demonstrations. Even though the anti-government protest was organized by students, there were obviously many that were not. I was told that you were a worker, were there many like you?" Vera continues her interview. "Maybe, but we did not see any difference between us, the goal was the same." "Is the violence still fresh in your memory, or is it being slowly forgotten?" "Life makes us gradually forget things that were at time of a great importance or difficult to overcome. But some events just do not fade away easily. If it is violence or peace, some happenings are constantly reconstructed in our memories. Like legends, they stay with us and we will always remember them." Patrick answers. "Could love be one of the unforgotten legends?" Vera asks with a gentle flirt on her lips. "Is it the Love, that timeless universal truth of the eternal and infinite?" laughs Patrick with a little twitch on his lips. Vera is enchanted by his response but after a few more questions there is not much more to ask. The interview is visibly over. She switches the voice recording, takes a couple of photos of Patrick, gives him a big smile and starts to write in her notebook.

The twitch of his lips, it is just like a sense of freedom, the lost meaning of life that is found. You will always remember that. It is like a single leaf on the tree you just happen to look at. An ordinary leaf and then a light breeze blows on it, making it move slightly and beautifully in the way you always remember. It is the feeling of freedom you get, walking through your dark cave of ignorance when suddenly a bright stripe of sunlight begins to lighten your path. You will always remember that.

Visibly bored, Patrick looks around the café. A woman just came in and is about to sit at the empty round table next to them. She is now ordering coffee and looks nostalgically through the window towards the National Theater. A crowd of people is waiting in the front of the theater to be let in. The show is about to start. Patrick and Vera smile at each other again and chat a bit. But his eyes keep constantly looking away from Vera to the next table where the woman is now drinking her coffee. She too seems to glance towards him once a while. Patrick enjoys her glimpses and keeps looking at her until their eyes suddenly meet. For a moment they stay that way and Patrick gets the shivers. "Would you excuse me for a moment to greet a friend?" he turns to Vera and steps towards the woman at the next table who is still looking at him. "Adella, is that you? It's unbelievable, after all these years!" he almost shouts with excitement. "Forgive me." he calms down extending his hands to her, "Remember me? I am Patrick, a bit older one, but still Patrick". "I recognized you Wilhelm, you did not change much." Adella says still shocked by such a surprise, reaching for his hand. "And I am happy you still remember my nickname." "You have always been only Wilhelm to me", says Adella, unable to hide her emotions now. "Can I introduce you to my companion?" wonders Patrick after a moment of just starring at her. "Please do." It is just two steps to the next table. The piano man still plays the background music beautifully, now it is the Beethoven's Moon Sonata. Patrick moves a third chair to their table and they start to chat together, mostly about politics and life and Vera's upcoming book. They are an interesting triangle. Their recollections of the past mingle together in a strange story that contains their pains and pleasures, sadness and laughter. A reconstruction of ordinary lives, one may think. It is fun to pick up the old memories but the present interrupts. Adella has to go. She pays for her coffee but before excusing herself, she insists that both of them come to the opening art show of her painter friend. "It is this Saturday at 2 pm, please come, it will be a great show, I promise." says she looking alternatively to Vera's and Patrick's eyes. Patrick accepts eagerly, but Vera has a lecture and a party she is obliged to attend, so she cannot make it. The women say goodbyes to each other with certain sadness. There seems to be some invisible tie between them, something that makes women of any background to understand each other. "All of us women are sisters," Vera says to Adella "and we will always be". "Then, we must be a priori soul mates", adds Adella with a smile and looks quickly from Vera's eyes to Patrick's. His eyes do not reciprocate the tenderness in hers; he is ready to walk her to the exit. The happy voices of the café packed with people are the only music that sounds in the space now. The piano man is taking a short break.

The art show is held in a small gallery under the Prague Castle. Petrsky's paintings are abstract and poetic at the same time. "Do you like this one?" he asks Patrick pointing to a red and black painting with a streak of blue painted metal on it. "Adella told me once, when we walked by the brook near my studio, she is going to keep a bit of water from it in her pocket to always remember that day. What a poetry! I bet you, buddy, that she still carries the memory in her pocket today. I reconstructed that memory and made a painting about it, this one. I call it Sound of Water and it is dedicated to her." He kisses Adella on the cheek and shakes Patrick's hand. "Take good care of her, buddy." "The picture is yours my lady, after the show." "You are my alchemist; love you my friend and thank you."Adella whispers into her friend's ear and smiles.

Patrick and Adella leave the exhibit and take a long walk from the Prague Castle towards the Charles Bridge and the Kampa Park. It is a pretty ordinary gloomy afternoon of the late fall with traces of the mostly melted snow on the ground. The sun pierces through the heavy clouds once a while making the world a little brighter. It is about an hour before the sunset. The shaggy lawn in the park is yellow-brown and a bit muddy but many people and dogs walk or run across it. Children are playing soccer, the muddy ball rolls around with pieces of yellow turf on it. The silvery water of the Devil Brook on one side of the park is fast moving, soon to enter the wide river Vltava on its other side. It is all the magic Prague can offer on this Saturday afternoon. The two of them, contrary to the cheerful atmosphere around them, are less joyful and more serious. "Let's sit down here for a while." Patrick finds an old bench under the wide crown of the ancient oak of which the brown falling leaves are gently setting on the ground. He pushes away those that landed on the bench and they make themselves comfortable. Strangely, they face away from the river they both used to love so much and there is a large gap between them.

We had walk here often, thinks Patrick, our first kiss happened here. Adella moves a bit closer to him: "Do you remember when I found you in that electronic shop you have worked before my emigration? You were already sporting a beard, like you have today. We talked about present but did not mention anything from our past. We just looked at each other, knowing each other's thoughts." "You reached for my hand and told me how lucky I was to find love and family. It felt strange." says Patrick sadly. "You know, time runs fast and it changed us and there are new rules for us..." Adella interrupts the unwanted silence that followed Patrick's statement: "The old rules, we thought we had, had not really been rules. It was only our rebellion against the rules. You know that it was a thrilling game and we were happy that way. Of course, it is all gone today, but I do not think about new rules. We just met today much grown up and living away from each other for such a long time but I still sense the almost same connection between us. Yet, I understand that if you kiss me now, my blood will not run fast through my veins and create that adrenaline I fell with almost every kiss when we were young. I will not smell that scent of wild roses spreading around me and will not see the deep universe in your eyes. I am sure that I will not feel the weight of the dust from the distant space falling slowly on my eyelids as I close my eyes. That magic is gone; gone forever." she says longingly with a bit of regret in her voice but still smiling at him. "It is just a memory, a nice memory. We are older now to feel that way." says Patrick. "We are, and the magic cannot happen again. We both have adapted to the life away from the life we used to know," jumps back in Adella. "I understand that. We are different; a bit older, maybe a little richer by something and a little poorer by something else, that's how it goes. We must adapt to it." adds Patrick. "And every new sunrise brings with it the concern about our aging. Even now, meeting after all these years with curiosity about each other, it is our age that creates this protective wall between us, like a security of the locked gate," says she a bit more excitedly, "but on the other hand, one cannot live at the premise that one is old and programming self to some kind of established reality, some life infrastructure, no matter how logical and convenient it may seem to be now. One should not stop searching for a new path that may lead to some discovery, new adventure or change of self. One has to adapt to some requirements that life is imposing on us and I do. But with that, I still want to break that uniform pattern, that structure and to rebel against the security of my age. I still want to find that path, that space of magic, that shiver, that desire, the scent of wild roses and that dust from the distant universe. I'll never forget that moment." Patrick turns his face to her: "I remember that too. That time, I wished our relationship had never ended. At times, I have hoped for its return". Adella looks directly to his eyes that are now little red and watery: "For a long time after, I have still wished that it ended differently". Patrick swings his legs over the bench and turns towards river Vltava, looking away from Adella. "We all had some wishes that did not come true or they took a long time to be fulfilled. I had carried many of such in my head and my heart, for freedom, for example. I have always known I was free in my heart and soul despite the situation outside of me. Some things had not work for me, some did". "I think both of our hearts were filled up with hopes for freedom and truth in those gloomy melancholic days, that we did not have there much space left for our loving. But you probably did not feel much love for me in the first place, did you?" asks Adella, looking away from the river and Patrick. "I did feel a lot for you those days, but stood aside and kept silent." Patrick says. "And I was waiting for you, Wilhelm" she turns towards Patrick, "to make your lion leap or just to get a little closer, to tell me how you feel about me, to ask me whom I really loved." Long silence follows Adella's remark. She turns around and looks towards the river. "I am so happy we ran into each other. I have always been looking for you, here and everywhere. But now, the meeting with the past and talking about it is difficult for me. It makes me feel sad to recollect my youth with its mistakes and decisions that went wrong. Yet, to carry the past locked up in my mind without saying a word about it would be worse. It would make the past disappear with no relation to the present. But I know that our kind of love was like a legend, an extraordinary love, so it must be remembered; it must be revealed; it must be passed on no matter how reconstructed it may come out. The past must be the part of our present. We needed to find each other and talk." Adella exclaims still with a bit of pathos in her voice. "It will be remembered." Patrick turns sideways to look into her eyes. "But the life goes on with new rules, our every day duties, schedules, small pleasures here and there. The patterns of these reconstructions are like memory puzzles. Sometimes a piece fits, sometimes it does not. The algorithms of the present time often points out to different strategies. Our children need us and we need them. They recharge our old energy to keep us going the way we are now. We need to be content with what it is now."

"That may be true, but there is more to life than just duties, children or the daily routines. There is always an entry to something new, something exciting not just these peaceful walks leading towards the end, the exit from life. The charges of energy you talk about do not come just from the outside or others. More importantly, they also come from the inside of us. Those are the dreams and wishes carried in the heart and mind, yet not fulfilled, still buried, waiting for their realization. There is still time to unbury them and there is still time to realize them… I have to do it! I will be searching for those forgotten dreams wherever they are on the land or in the sea."

They look at each other for a long time without saying a word. It is close to sunset but the sun does not shine. It manages to peek out of the clouds for a minute and is gone. They get up from the bench at the same time. Holding hands, they are walking slowly and silently, like shy teenagers in love, out of the park. They found each other at last. They used to be soul mates. Like a brother and sister, they eventually grew apart. It is just the last hug and kisses on the cheeks. "And if you reach the ocean, Adella... please ...tell my best regards..." Patrick turns his face towards her. "I will call your name into the waves... Wilhelm ... I promise." Adella says to Patrick looking for the last time into his eyes.

They will be living apart, separated by time and space yet still connected by their memories. There is no wall between them, just

the distance. Adella's airline ticket to an island in North Atlantic

is in her purse, her luggage is packed, just to be retrieved from the

hotel and ready to go. There is a new path on the way to an open

horizon and the space of magic. As she runs across the road to

catch the tram, the scent of wild roses overwhelms her senses and

the dust from the distant universe begins to fall on her lashes.

EPILOGUE

I am standing on the high cliff of Aran Island. "Wilhelm! Wilhelm! Wilhelm!" I am calling against the wind and into the loud noise of the wild waves of the Atlantic Ocean bellow. The name that carries in it my life story disappears as if sunk into the deep moving water of the powerful sea. It is gone, over. All such calls vanish like a bad memory, broken down by the rough swell on the top of the mass of the deep water. The going out tide is taking those powerful fragments of memory far away from me, but I know that with every wild tide coming in, reconstructed to a bare recollection, my calls will return to me. Like a gentle mist hovering above the ocean, they will stay in my head. Memory: a powerful entity.

ACKNOWLEDGEMENTS

There are many people whose companionship, love or friendships in the past and present time have been a source of my recollection, re-examination and inspiration for writing this book. Some of them had passed me briefly to remember their names, although their life stories touched me deeply and stayed imprinted in my memory. Others had even deeper impact on my life especially during the totalitarian regime of Czechoslovakia. Amongst those were my parents and grandparents whose actions were examples to me to live my life with honor and courage. My friend Vlasta Netrda had been an emotional support in the hardest times of the totalitarian era. In the USA, my Professor Harry Bober urged me to write. For that I am very grateful. I have been blessed by having the talented, creative and thoughtful son Gabriel Gold who has always inspired me. I give many thanks to

Eric Wilson for being there when I needed him, for being a willing listener and helping to prepare the book for publishing. I need to thank to my parents and grandparents who created for me a sweet childhood full of arts, music and literature. I am grateful that I grew up in the family that cherished love and truth above all. That has shaped the whole meaning of my life. I am ever thankful for such learning. Many thanks go to late President Vaclav Havel without whose effort and victory for the peace and democracy I would never be able to visit my birthplace again or write this book.

ABOUT THE AUTHOR

 Alena was born in Prague, Czech Republic. Because of her family activism during the totalitarian era of the former Czechoslovakia she was denied entry to higher education and was initially trained as an electro mechanic. Striving to educate herself, she was nevertheless able to complete the evening School of Economy and Mechanical Engineering. Like her father, she loved painting and attended private painting lessons with a well known Czech painter.

In 1978, during the harsh politics of the authoritarian regime and prosecutions of those involved in the human rights movement Charta 77, Alena emigrated from Czechoslovakia to Vienna,

Austria and was shortly admitted to the United States, receiving US citizenship. She pursued her further education in New York City where she received her bachelor's degree in Art History and Psychology from Hunter College, master's degree in Art History and Archeology from NYU. She also studied for a postgraduate degree in Arizona State University. Alena was a writer and volunteer in the New York City Mayor's public sculpture survey and served in the Phoenix - Prague Sister Cities. She has worked as a freelance writer and translator and art curator.

Alena lives alternatively in the beautiful Cannon Beach, Oregon, USA and the magical Prague, Czech Republic.